Fast!

To Professor Doctor Auntie Gail

**Thanks, as always, to my away team: Joan and Kristen;
and to my home team: Jason, Beck, Tia, Tatum, and Kelley!**

Faster! Faster!

Leslie Patricelli

CANDLEWICK PRESS

Faster!

Faster!

Faster! Faster!

Faster! Faster!

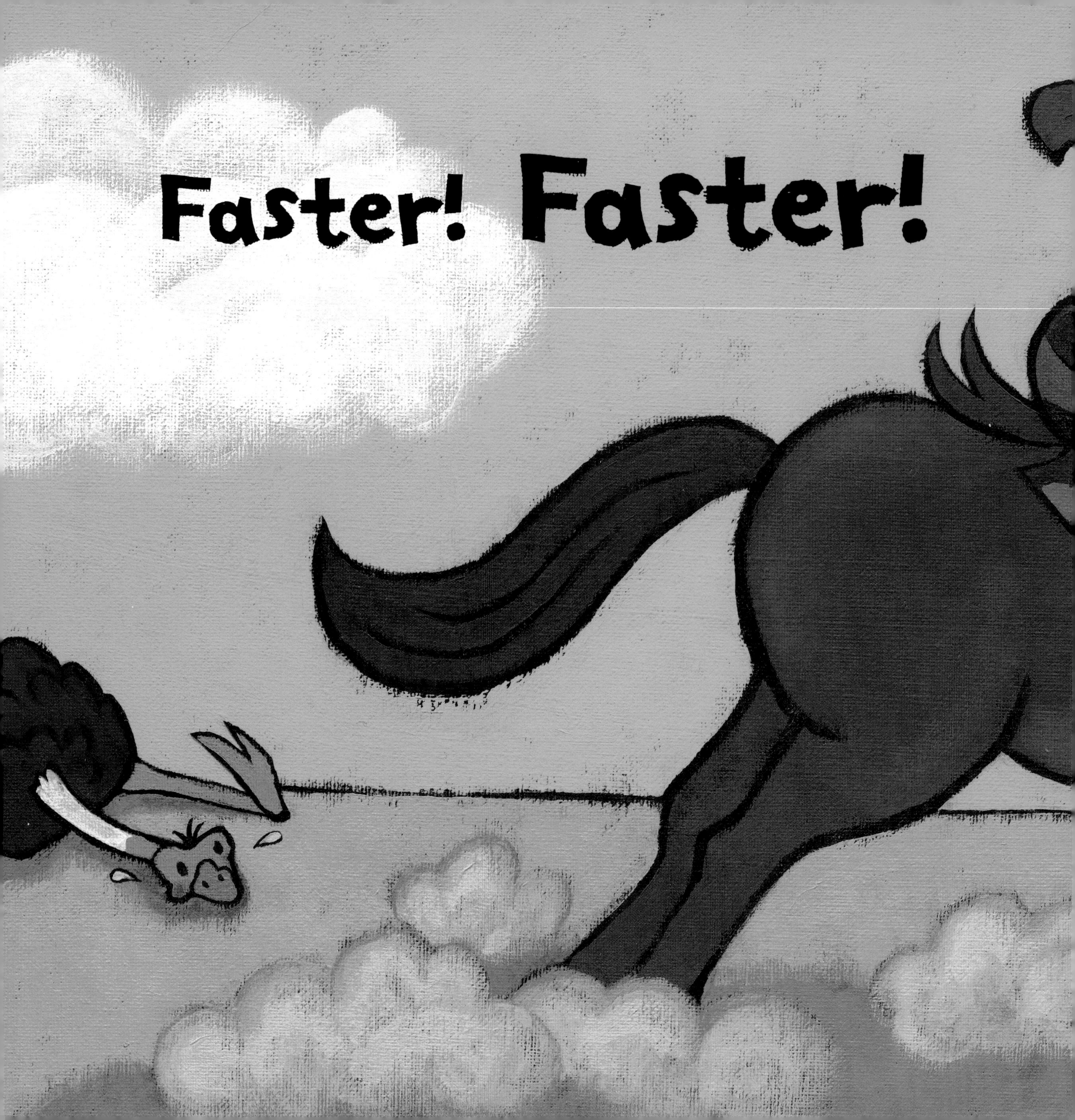

Faster!

Faster! Faster!

You're fast,
Daddy!